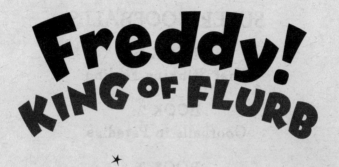

Freddy!
KING OF FLURB

Books by PETER HANNAN

Freddy! King of Flurb
Freddy! Deep-Space Food Fighter

SUPER GOOFBALLS

Freddy! KING OF FLURB

Written and Illustrated by

PETER HANNAN

HARPER
An Imprint of HarperCollinsPublishers

Library of Congress Cataloging-in-Publication Data
Hannan, Peter.
Freddy! King of Flurb / written and illustrated by Peter
Hannan. — 1st ed.
    p.   cm.
Summary: Freddy, his jealous sister Babette, and their
parents are abducted by slimy aliens and taken to the planet
Flurb, where Freddy is made king, much to the dismay of
Wizbad.
ISBN 978-0-06-128466-3
[1. Human-alien encounters—Fiction. 2. Brothers
and sisters—Fiction. 3. Jealousy—Fiction. 4. Family
life—Fiction. 5. Kings, queens, rulers, etc.—Fiction.
6. Humorous stories.]   I. Title.
PZ7.H1978Fre   2011   2010018442
[Fic]—dc22   CIP
                                            AC

Typography by Alison Klapthor
11 12 13 14 15   CG/CW   10 9 8 7 6 5 4 3 2 1
❖
First Edition

For Tom and Jill

★ CONTENTS ★

1

FREDDY, KING OF ZILCH

Why was Freddy first in line at Greasy King that Saturday morning? Why did he drink twenty-seven humungo-sized root beers for breakfast? It wasn't because he wanted the twenty-seven cardboard Greasy King crowns they gave him. It wasn't because he wanted to win the First Annual

I Was a Big Pig at Greasy King Contest. It wasn't even because he liked root beer so much.

No, the reason goes way back. Three semesters ago, his sister, Babette, decided that it would be fun to get to the mailbox early and be the first to see the report cards. Then she pulled them out at the dinner table and read them aloud in front of the whole family.

"Let's see here, semester one . . . English: Babette . . . A plus. And Freddy . . . awwww . . . C plus."

"Well," said Freddy, "they're both *pluses*."

"Very amusing, Freddy," said Babette. "But let's check out the comments. This one's from Mrs. Gizby: 'There are a few wonderful students who make teaching worthwhile. And then there is Babette, whose amazing wonderfulness dwarfs the regular wonderfulness of those other students.'"

"Gee, that's a nice one," said Mom.

"You think?" said Babette. "Okay, now let's check out a comment about young Freddy. Here goes: 'Are we absolutely sure that Freddy is Babette's brother? Could there have been a mix-up at the hospital? Sincerely, Mrs. Frumpkiss.'"

"Mrs. Frumpkiss is nuts," said Freddy.

"She hates *everyone*."

"That's funny," said Dad. "She loved Babette."

"Like I said," said Freddy, "she's nuts."

WHAT A CARD

The next semester, Freddy tried to beat Babette to the mailbox, but she met the mailman a block from their house. And then *this* Saturday she walked to the post office and greeted the mailman before he even left on his route.

But this time Freddy was prepared. You see . . . Freddy is a funny-noise specialist. He makes noises with his mouth, nose, hands, armpits, feet, and several other body parts. If there were an Olympics for excellence in noise-ology, Freddy would have a roomful of gold medals.

Drinking all that root beer had been part of Freddy's grand plan. When he got home, he quickly dragged his microphone and amplifier from the basement. He positioned the amp near the front gate, hidden by the hedge.

"Testing . . . one, two, three," whispered Freddy. The amp crackled and buzzed.

Then Freddy waited and waited and finally heard Babette returning from the post office, her footsteps echoing on the sidewalk from halfway down the block.

Louder footsteps, the clank of the front

gate, the first sight of her shoe around the corner of the hedge and . . . Freddy let 'er rip.

First he did the Bionic Belch: *"BURRR-EEP-EEP-EEP-BLAMMO!"* Then the Gassy Whistle: *"TWEET-TWEET-ZZZZZOP-HOOTY-HOOT-KABOOM!"* And finally his specialty—the Squawking, Flapping, Atomic-Raspberry-Chicken Salute. Freddy jumped around with eyes rolling and arms flapping. He made sounds that seemed unmakeable for a human.

And they were loud . . . very, very loud. The entire neighborhood shook.

Babette screamed and fell into the hedge. The mail exploded in all directions.

A tiny worm poked its head out of the lawn, screamed, and then dived back into the soil.

Freddy quickly scooped up the report cards and ran.

Dad threw open the screen door. "What was that?!" he grumbled.

"Only the best Atomic-Raspberry-Chicken Salute *ever*,"

said Mom from the kitchen window.

Freddy's mother always said that her love for Freddy was infinite. She hardly ever got mad at him. His father had no such trouble. He had a real talent for getting mad.

Babette walked into the house. "When I rule the world," she sneered, "Freddy will *definitely* not be in it."

"Okay by me," said Freddy with a smile, "but you seem to have dropped these." He held up two report cards.

Babette snatched the cards from his hand. The whole family gathered around not knowing Freddy had replaced *this* semester's report cards with *last* semester's report cards, which he had carefully altered.

"Okay . . . let's hear about me first," she said, "since I am first in every way."

She opened the envelope.

"Oh, goody," said Babette, "a comment about me from Mr. English." She imitated Mr. English, the English teacher, who spoke in a fake English accent. "'Unfortunately, this semestah has proven to be a total disastah for Babette. D plus.' WHAT?!"

"At least it's a plus!" said Freddy.

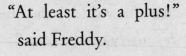

Babette's face twisted into a grimace. "'Please call to schedule a conference! Since she is incapable of handling the material, I recommend holding her back a year . . . or two?!'"

It took a whole

wonderful fifteen seconds for Babette and their parents to figure out what had happened. Dad pointed at Freddy and then to the stairs and growled. Freddy went to bed early. But it was worth it.

INTRUDER

Freddy woke up. He heard a creak ... or a squeak. And then a few noises that sounded mechanical and yet voicelike.

Zeeeeeeeeeep.

Grooooooooda-doink.

Yee-eeeeeeeeeeee-
bahhh-yeeeee.

Someone was outside his window. He grabbed the Wiffle bat that he kept next to his bed and, in one swift ninja-like motion, he vaulted himself in the air.

But he didn't land with the thwack of bare feet on hardwood floor that he'd expected. No thwack. No nothing.

He looked down and realized he was hovering about two feet up. He had suddenly acquired the ability to defy gravity. Was he dreaming? Then a bunch of green tentacles covered with eyeballs came *through* the walls, as if the wood, plaster, wallpaper, and movie posters were

made of liquid. The tentacles wriggled
and wound their way around the furniture,
eyeballs rolling and blinking, checking
things out.

"Ummm . . . excuse me, whatever
you are," said Freddy. "What exactly are
you looking for?"

One of the tentacles snapped to attention

like a cobra. It moved close to Freddy's face. On its tip was a mouth and the mouth opened.

"We are looking for exactly *you*," it whispered.

All of a sudden another tentacle's mouth opened much wider and started sucking like a vacuum cleaner—an extremely powerful one. Freddy was being pulled in. He tried swimming in the air in the opposite direction, but he got slurped in like a piece of spaghetti.

"No . . . ahhhhh . . . ooooooof!" he said.

The same thing was happening to

Freddy's parents in their room.

"No . . . ahhhhh . . . oooooof!" said Mom.

"What?! What?! . . . No . . . ahhhh . . . oooooooof!" grumbled Dad.

And in Babette's room: "How *dare* you!" she squawked. "No . . . ahhhhh . . . oooooof!"

4

WELCOME ABOARD

Freddy passed helplessly through the cramped passageway and got shot out like a wad of paper through a straw. He slammed against a wall and slid to the ground. The rest of the family came flying out next and slid to a stop next to him. Everyone was covered with tentacle-passageway glop.

"That was the grossest thing since Freddy

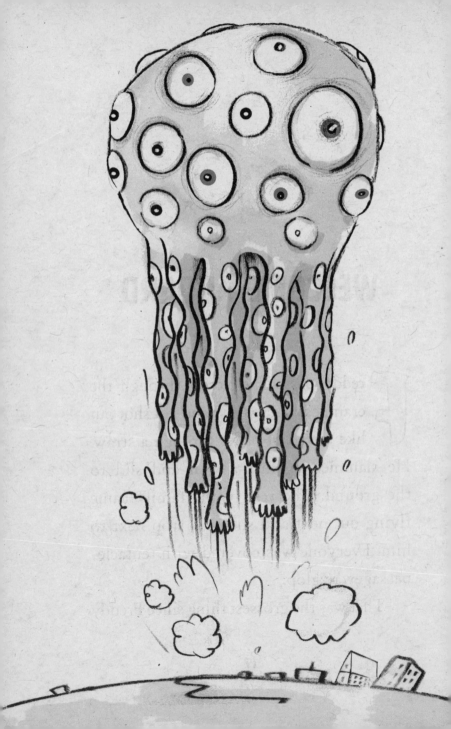

was born," said Babette.

Freddy used his hand like a squeegee to de-glop his face. He looked around. He could see through the walls and he saw the houses and trees of his neighborhood getting smaller and smaller. "Abducted," Freddy said softly as Earth fell away.

Babette was still de-glopping her eyes.

"What are you mumbling about *now*?" she said.

"Oh, nothing," said Freddy, "just that we've been abducted."

"Don't be silly," she said. "Who on Earth would want to abduct *us*?"

"That's just it—they're not *on Earth*," said Freddy, "and neither are we anymore."

Mom's, Dad's, and Babette's eyes popped open wide. Then they screamed at the top of their lungs.

5

SPACED

"Listen up, whoever the heck is driving this monstrosity," barked Dad. "I have to be at work tomorrow morning!"

"And the *prom* is tomorrow *night!*" screamed Babette.

"*Bleezer goiterbeeber gloxoid,*" said a super-calm, super-low voice. "Oh, sorry, English. Might as well settle in—we've got

a sixty-two-million-light-year drive ahead of us."

Babette glared at Freddy. "I blame you for this."

They were moving so fast, the stars and planets looked like chalk lines against the blackness of space. All was quiet and the family dropped off to sleep. Turns out, being abducted is quite exhausting.

IMPACT

Freddy opened one eye slowly and realized that the ship was nearing a planet. It looked like a lime-green gum ball, but it was growing quickly like a film in fast motion. Freddy woke his family and it occurred to all of them at exactly the same moment that they were about to crash.

They closed their eyes, gritted their teeth,

and prepared to be flattened like pancakes.

But the planet's surface opened up and the ship went *into* it instead of smashing *onto* it. Then it closed behind them, like they'd been swallowed.

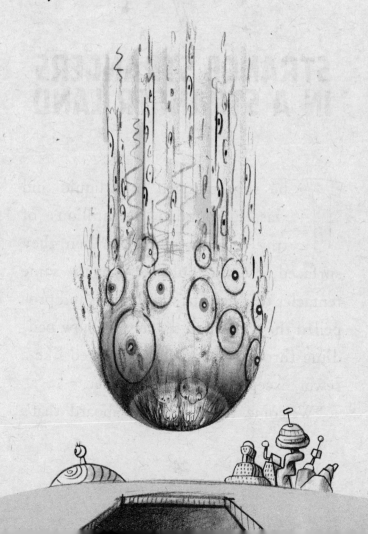

7

STRANGE STRANGERS IN A STRANGER LAND

The ship plunged into liquid and was surrounded by millions of tiny orange bubbles. When they surfaced, Freddy could see that the same tentacles that had sucked them in and propelled them through space were now paddling through a tunnel that looked like a sewer, except much, much fancier.

"Welcome to Flurb! All aboard that's

going ashore!" said the ship, pulling up to the dock. "And that means *you*, the Freddy and the Freddy's family!"

"How does it even know your name?" said Mom.

"The real question," grumbled Dad, "is why, when I'm the leader of the family, did they single Freddy out like that?"

"That's obvious," said Babette. "Freddy is such a screwup, such a loser, such a twerp dork ignoramus, he's finally gotten us *all* into trouble . . . with the entire universe."

Freddy didn't want to admit it, but he was thinking the exact same thing.

A large door slid open. The Flurbian military lined the dock and waved their many arms—if they were in fact all arms—signaling the family to exit the ship.

"Oh, no, I am *not* going out there!" said Babette.

But just then the walls of the cabin started pushing inward, bunching the family closer and closer together and squeezing them out into a pile on the dock like toothpaste squished from a tube.

The alien soldiers—or whatever they were— roared like velociraptors, only nastier.

"*GREEEE-ORRRRR-REEEEEEK!*"

ALL FREDDY'S FAULT

Babette shut her eyes and repeated three words over and over through clenched teeth. "All Freddy's fault, all Freddy's fault, all Freddy's fault . . ."

"Okay, okay," said Freddy, "it's my fault." He tried to stand up, but his face immediately slammed back onto the dock. "Flurb's gravitational pull is obviously much stronger than Earth's."

"Nonsense!" snapped Dad. He pushed himself up and onto his feet in one quick motion and then belly flopped hard onto the dock. "I'd rather lie down anyway," he grumbled.

One alien guard leaned in toward Freddy. *"GREEEEEE-ORRRRR-REEEEEEK!"* he roared, blowing hot breath into Freddy's face like a very smelly furnace. It stung like a sunburn.

There must have been some kind of anti-gravity ray in the guard's breath, because Freddy floated off the ground. The alien turned and walked, and Freddy floated behind him.

Mom leaped and grabbed his legs. Dad grabbed *her* legs, and Babette grabbed *his*. All this had absolutely no effect, except that now the entire family was floating along.

THE GRAND HALL OF FLURBISHNESS

They passed through a high-arched entranceway. The rest of the aliens from the dock followed and let out that same angry-sounding screech—*GREEEEEE-ORRRRR-REEEEEEK*—convincing the family that they were indeed being delivered to their doom.

Babette shrieked.

Mom's lip trembled. "Al! Do something!"

"Darn right I will!" growled Dad. Just then a tiny eggplant-shaped Flurbian shot his long ropelike fingers up and around Dad's head, covering his mouth, and shutting him up.

They moved through a hallway that seemed to be breathing, like it was part of a larger living thing. Weird aliens peered down at them from little windows in the walls. A Flurbian child pointed at Babette and laughed.

"HEY!" screamed Babette, "WHERE I COME FROM I AM A VERY IMPORTANT PERSON!"

This made the Flurbian child laugh his head off. But then he just put it back on and laughed some more.

"That's odd, Babette," said Freddy. "You never had a sense of humor on *Earth*."

Suddenly, they heard the murmur of a crowd up ahead. The hallway turned and opened into the Grand Hall of Flurbishness.

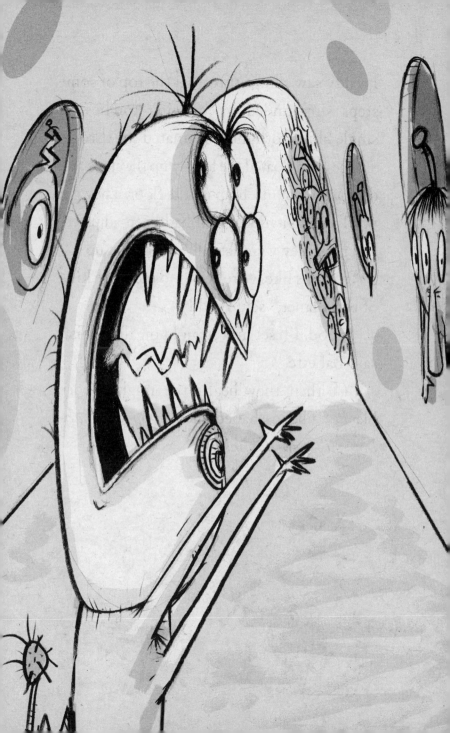

Freddy saw a huge throne at the top of some steps surrounded by burning torches. A single blue spotlight illuminated the throne.

The alien floated the family up the steps and dumped them in a heap on the floor. They got up. The gravitational pull had been adjusted, and now they were actually *able* to get up.

"It looks like we're about to meet the king of this planet," said Freddy.

"Good. I'll set him straight on all of this," said Babette.

Just then they heard the mighty horn blast of a horn-shaped alien—*bop-pah-pah-bop-pah-pah-pahhhhhh!*

WIZBAD AND GLYZIX

All the Flurbians instantly dropped to their knees or whatever they had to drop to. The entire family followed along . . . kneeling, bowing, arms out in front, doing that typical worshipping motion.

Two figures approached. The first was a multicolored creature with at least three eyeballs, but who's counting. Actually, it was

impossible to count, because he was juggling them. He seemed to be an entertainer, like a court jester. His head had a bunch of plumes sticking out that weren't exactly feathers, but more like floppy extensions of his scalp. He didn't walk—he hopped. His body telescoped in and out of itself, making a slurpy suction sound. Basically, he was a living, breathing, juggling, jumping jack-in-the-box. The crowd loved him.

The other guy was a lot less lovable. *Horrifying* was more like it. He was dressed in a royal sort of way and he looked almost human, except he had a glowing wand growing out of his bald noggin. He had sickly yellow eyes and one razor-sharp fang, which he was sharpening with a small file. He glared at Freddy and hissed, *"GORREEX-BABBA!"*

"I get the feeling," said Freddy, "that

Wand Head here just said something like I hate your guts."

"*GORREEX-BABBA-BABBA!*" roared Wand Head.

"Make that I hate your guts and would be delighted to murder you immediately," said Freddy.

Wand Head stepped toward Freddy but tripped and landed fang first on the floor.

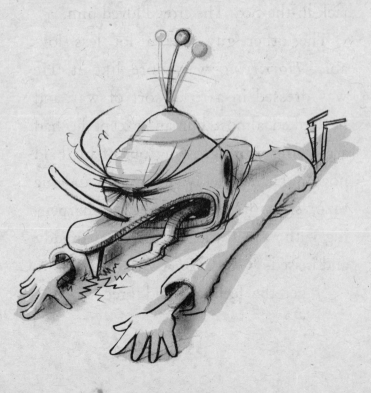

A few Flurbians chuckled, but Wand Head pried his fang out, spun around, and made a face so mean that three aliens in the front row burst into flames. Two others melted. One wet his pants.

Wand Head motioned to the juggling alien, who hopped and slurped toward the family. He slapped a pair of antennae onto each family member's head.

The antennae sparked and popped.

"Oooo," said Mom, "now *that* feels weird."

"Feels like something weird is happening to my *brain*," said Freddy.

"It could only be an improvement in your case," said Babette, but then she felt the same weird feeling. "Hold on . . . this is *not funny*! *My* brain is actually *worth something*!"

"Remind-eth me to melt it down and sell-est it," sneered Wand Head. Amazingly, the family understood what he was saying. The antennae were translators. "I be-est Wizbad, the royal wizard," he continued. "Glyzix, bring-eth me the Freddy and the family of the Freddy."

The colorful little jester hopped and slurped in a circle, herding them toward Wizbad.

WHAT NEXT?

reddy and his family huddled close together and Wizbad glared down at them. The room got deadly silent.

Wizbad pointed one of his long, bony fingers and a ring of light shot over the top of Freddy's head and encircled his body. It lifted Freddy and positioned him in the air above the throne. Apparently Flurbians never got bored with seeing people float in the air.

The alien band struck up a tune.

The band grew louder and louder and then suddenly stopped.

"Greetings, Earth nerd," Wizbad whispered so only Freddy could hear. "I hate-est your guts . . ."

". . . and you would be delighted to kill-eth me immediately?" said Freddy.

"No," continued Wizbad. "I would be delighted to kill-eth you slowly and *painfully*. But I can't because of the stupid royal decree from Ex-king Wormola before he retired-eth to fish-eth for space trout. Somehow, that old *fool*—I mean our *beloved ex-leader*—found you *most suitable* to be-est exalted ruler of Flurb. Even though I was the obvious choice—the second in command, the one with the cool head wand, the good looks, and the winning personality!"

Wizbad was in quite a state. He was trembling with such anger that his head wand vibrated back and forth like a high-speed windshield wiper, shooting sparks in all directions.

"Well, Mr. Wizbad, sir," said Freddy, "as far as I'm concerned, you can have the throne. I wouldn't mind just going home."

"Oh, you wouldn't mind just going home?! Well, *I* wouldn't mind grinding you into Earth nerd paste!" spluttered Wizbad. "However, once Ex-king Wormola declare-est you king, that's it . . . you're *king*! But, mark my words . . . I will claim-est the throne if I have to chew-eth you up and spit-eth you down a black hole to do it!"

Wizbad reached into the pocket of his coat and pulled out a jewel-studded crown. He held it tenderly, kissing and caressing it for a moment, and then gently rolled it off the tips of his fingers. It rotated slowly in the air and settled upright, hovering above Freddy's head.

Wizbad wiped the sweat from his brow and forced himself to say what he didn't want to say. His voice echoed through the huge hall: "ALL RIGHT, DO YOU, THE ONE THEY

CALL-ETH FREDDY, PROMISE TO SERVE-ETH AND PROTECT-ETH THE CITIZENS OF FLURB? TO FULFILL-ETH YOUR DUTIES, AND BLAH, BLAH, BLAH-ETH?"

"Could you define *blah-eth*?" said Freddy.

"JUST SAY *YES*!"

"Umm . . ." said Freddy nervously, "yes?"

"THEN," Wizbad continued, his face contorting into the most pained, insincere smile ever, "BY THE POWER VESTED IN ME, I HEREBY CROWN-ETH THEE . . . FREDDY, KING OF FLURB!"

Wizbad blinked hard, and the crown slammed down onto Freddy's head.

"Ouch!" said Freddy.

"YAYYYY!" cheered the Flurbians.

"*Bop-pah-pah-bop-pah-pah-pahhhhhh!*" blasted the horn alien.

"YIPPEEE!" squealed Mom.

"YOU HAVE *GOT* TO BE *KIDDING*!" shrieked Babette and Dad.

The crowd leaped to its feet and did the Squawking, Flapping, Atomic-Raspberry-Chicken Salute.

THE FLURBIAN
ANTHEM

Was this some kind of cosmic joke? All the aliens bowed down and chanted. "Freeeeeeeeeeedd-yyyyyyyyy! Freeeeeeeeeeddyyyyyyyyy! Freeeeeeeeeeddyyyyyyyyy!"

Glyzix telescoped up over the crowd.

"Attention, good citizens of Flurb," he said. "It's time to sing the new official anthem!"

"Who's the kid, from far away,
From some boring little burb?
Got a kingdom, he's here to stay . . .
It's Freddy, the King of Flurb!

"Brave leader, there's no doubt . . .
No crisis can disturb,
The crowd's excited, hear them shout:
Hail, Freddy . . . the King of Flurb!

"The King of Flurb, oh what a job,
You know it takes a lotta nerve,
Can't be no slacker, can't be no slob,
I'm talking Freddy, the King of Flurb!"

"B o p - p a h - p a h - b o p - p a h - p a h -
pahhhhhh!" blasted the horn alien again,
and everyone threw something like confetti
into the air, only it was wet and smelled like
mold or fish . . . or moldy fish. A huge, soggy
clump of this glop landed on Babette's head.

But she didn't even notice, because she was in a deep state of shock. Her screwed up, annoying, immature, irritating little brother was now the boss of an entire planet. And the boss of *her*. She reacted in a perfectly logical way. She staggered a bit and dropped dead.

13

FAMILY TURMOIL

"**N**ooo!" said Mom and Dad.

"Ouch *again*," said Freddy. Babette had fallen on his toe.

"King Freddy, are you all right?!" shrieked Glyzix.

"I'm fine," said Freddy.

"Thank goodness," said Glyzix. "Luckily she's dead—she was dangerous, attacking your royal toe like that."

"Poor Babette just fainted," said Mom.

"Oh," said Glyzix. "Well, then she's *still* dangerous. Arrest the one they call Poor Babette!"

The guards leaped upon Babette, which was easy since she had fainted and wasn't moving or anything. They lifted her above their heads and started hauling her off to jail.

Freddy spoke up. "Stop! That's my sister! Put her down!"

They stopped dead in their tracks and dropped Babette. This woke her up.

"Wow," she said with a sigh of relief, "you will not

believe the ridiculous dream I had. Freddy was king!"

The roomful of Flurbians took this as a cue. "HAIL, FREDDY, KING OF FLURB!" they cheered.

Babette fainted again.

Dad was not exactly pleased either. He had never really been king of the castle on Earth, but he always *said* he was. And now that Freddy was the official glorious ruler of this new world, Dad felt a great grumpiness bubbling up inside him.

Mom felt different. "Freddy," she squealed, "I knew you'd go far. I didn't expect you to go *this* far . . . and I didn't think we'd all go *with* you . . . but still, I'm sure you'll make an adorable exalted ruler."

"Gee, thanks, Mom," said Freddy.

WHY?

Freddy turned to Glyzix and asked the obvious question: "Why *me*?"

"Well," said Glyzix, "Ex-king Wormola the nine hundred and ninety-ninth has watched you develop over the years and he liked what he saw. The State-Senator-Meets-Banana-Cream-Pie Incident; the Mrs. Frumpkiss-Bionic-Burp-O-Gram Incident; and just yesterday, the historic episode that

made his immediate retirement possible—the
Greasy-King-Report-Card Incident."

"He witnessed that?"

"Do you recall seeing a worm watching
you from the grass?"

"That teeny gray worm is king of this
planet?"

"*Was*,"
said Glyzix.
"You're king
now. And
Ex-king
Wormola was
a good king,
but the job
started to get
on his nerves."

"Why?"
said Freddy.

"Not sure,"

said Glyzix. "It's obviously the best job ever. Everyone loves you, your wishes are their commands, you get to live in a beautiful palace and do *whatever* you want *whenever* you want! So I have no idea—maybe it was the constant threat of death and destruction from Flurb's bloodthirsty neighbors?"

"Bloodthirsty neighbors?!" said Freddy.

"Sure, but don't worry," said Glyzix, "as they say, crossing the street is a lot more dangerous!"

"Really?" said Freddy.

"No"—Glyzix laughed—"that's just what they say. Bloodthirsty neighbors are *way* more dangerous. Plus, Wizbad is a pain in the you know what."

Freddy wondered what had happened to Wizbad, but then he spied the wizard standing in the shadows in a corner of the great hall. His glowing yellow eyes were intensely focused on Freddy. He was sharpening his fang so rapidly, it sounded like a dentist's drill. Sparks and bits of tooth exploded like tiny fireworks around his mouth. Sickly green steam billowed from his ears.

"To tell you the truth," said Freddy, "I can sorta understand why he'd be upset. He *was* second in command and everything."

"He's *still* second in command, so he hasn't lost a thing," said Glyzix. "Look, Kingster, Wormola wanted you, so you got the job. When the job gets on *your* nerves,

Wizbad can take over. He's just gotta be a little patient."

"He doesn't look like the patient type," said Freddy.

Wizbad's face had turned the color of a pomegranate, and his ear steam swirled around his head like a storm cloud. Freddy heard a deep rumbling.

"Is that thunder?" he said.

"No," said Glyzix. "That's Wizbad's stomach growling. He is very hungry . . . for revenge. The hunger surges up through his internal organs and vents out of his ears. One of these days, I'm expecting a full-blown eruption—ash, lava, flaming boulders, the works. It's an evil wizard thing."

Wizbad slunk into a dark passageway. He marched through one of Flurb's many tunnels—shoulders hunched and fists clenched. He wheezed heavily; and the tunnel, part of Flurb's living architecture, wheezed along with him. Wizbad chanted rhythmically with his footsteps: "I HATE-ETH THE FREDDY. I HATE-ETH THE FREDDY. I HATE-ETH THE FREDDY."

WHAT ABOUT US?

In the great hall, Freddy smiled at his subjects.

"Hail, Freddy, King of Flurb!" they screamed, like he was a huge rock star.

"Isn't it *wonderful*!" said Mom.

"It's just *peachy*, Miriam," said Dad. "Freddy gets to be king. But what the heck do *we* get to do?"

"You've all been chosen for super-important

governmental positions," said Glyzix. "Just follow Zeeb here, the friendly Flurbian employment supervisor."

Supervisor Zeeb was a large, powerful-looking, square-jawed robot.

"Right this way, Poor Babette, Peachy Miriam, and . . . excuse me, who are you?" said Supervisor Zeeb.

"I'm only Freddy's *father*!" snapped Dad.

"Well, right this way to you too, Only Freddy's Father!" said Zeeb as he led them through a door.

"Are they going to be okay?" said Freddy.

"More than okay! They will love their new jobs!"

ON-THE-JOB COMPLAINING

The family walked for what seemed like ten miles to Freddy's royal living chamber. His bedroom was the size of a football field.

"Congratulations, Peachy Miriam," said Zeeb. "From this day forward, you will be known as Royal Crown Polisher!"

"Yippee!" said Mom.

"Yippee?" said Dad and Babette.

"When do I start?" said Mom.

"Right *now*, Peachy Miriam!" said Zeeb. He threw open a huge closet door, revealing dazzling crowns of every variety, more than you could count.

"Yippee!" said Mom again as she dived in and started polishing to her heart's content.

"And the one called Only Freddy's Father," said Supervisor Zeeb, opening the next closet, "*you* get to be Royal *Boot* Polisher! And here's a neat bit of trivia—there are exactly the same number of royal boots as stars in the galaxy!"

"I'm no boot polisher! I should be king!" growled Dad.

"HA, HA, HO, HO, HO!" laughed Zeeb, holding his sides. "That's a good one, Only Freddy's Father. Okeydokey . . . get buffing!"

Babette was at her breaking point.

"Don't even think about getting me to polish my brother's smelly boots!" she said.

"Royal smelly boot polishing is a job that most Flurbians would give their three or four right arms for! And *your* job is an even *greater* honor!" he said.

"Finally," said Babette, "a little respect."

Zeeb tied a funny little paper hat on Babette's head.

"I am pleased to inform you, Poor Babette, that you have been named Royal Boot *Licker*."

"Boot licker!? You must be joking!" said Babette. "Why would boots even *need* to be licked!"

"To see if they *taste* right," he said, leading her through the door to the bootlicking closet. "My word, Poor Babette, did you leave your brain in your other head?"

17

ROYAL STEED

Meanwhile, back in the Grand Hall of Flurbishness, Freddy was basking in the adoration of his subjects. A fan-faced Flurbian fanned him with her face, and another showered him with compliments like "Looking good, your highness! Looking great, your highness! Looking way better than anyone in this or any other universe, your highness!"

"Adoration feels good," said Freddy.

Another Flurbian popped delicious candies into Freddy's mouth.

"And it *tastes* even better," he said. "What do you call these?"

"Yootleturds," said Glyzix.

"Perfect," said Freddy.

Flurbian citizens were lined up out the door of the grand hall, anxious to bestow Freddy with gifts. He tried to open a strange little green package, but it turned out to be a living creature that just sort of unfolded itself.

"Hey. Puffspike here," it said. "Gee, King . . . you're so ugly, when you were born the doctor slapped the wrong end. And punched your mother. Heh, heh."

Glyzix shook his head and leaped high off the ground. He pulled his body inside itself and turned sideways in midair, then thrust his legs in a bizarre karate-like move, kicking Puffspike

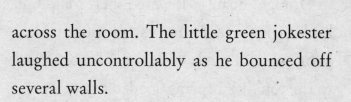

across the room. The little green jokester laughed uncontrollably as he bounced off several walls.

"There's something you don't see every day," said Freddy.

"Maybe not where you come from," said Glyzix.

Freddy realized that the room had gotten darker. He looked up to see a huge creature floating above him. It was bigger than an elephant. Bigger than *five* elephants. It was bright orange and had one gigantic blue eye.

"What the heck is *that*?" said Freddy.

"Orange Beauty, your royal steed," said Glyzix. "Time for a ride. One of your kingly duties is to have lots and lots and lots of fun. Uncontrollable laughter is valued above all else on Flurb."

Orange Beauty lowered her long tail, kinking it into right angles, forming an escalator, which Freddy rode up. Glyzix sprang to the top like a spring-loaded toy.

A huge skylight opened above them and although Orange Beauty was floating in the air, she reared back as if standing on her hind legs.

Glyzix whispered something to Freddy.

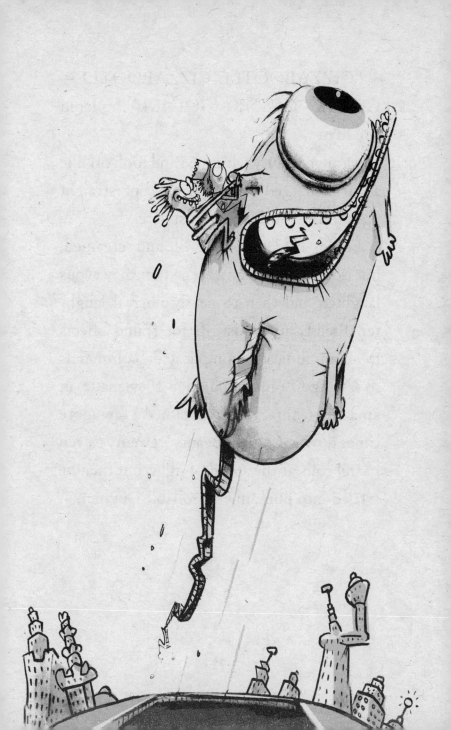

"GIZZABOOTLE, GIZZABOOTLE—GOINK, GOINK, GOINK!" hollered Freddy.

Orange Beauty whinnied and took off like a turbocharged racehorse—except straight up into the Flurbian stratosphere.

Freddy held on for dear life and screamed, but soon the scream turned into nervous laughter, and then to nearly normal laughter. Freddy used his gift for sound effects to communicate complicated commands to Orange Beauty, and soon they made an amazing team. Freddy screamed a few more times during Orange Beauty's twenty-seven barrel rolls at the speed of light, but then he settled into pure, uncontrollable laughter.

18

HENCH-SNAKES

Wizbad wasn't laughing though. He watched Freddy and Orange Beauty soar across the red Flurbian sky . . . and started sharpening his tooth again. He snapped his slimy fingers. A sliding door opened in the floor and from it floated a large glowing stone . . . Wizbad's wizard stone. The stone was his method of spying on citizens all over Flurb. He stared into it and was deeply disturbed by what he saw: Flurbians looking happy. He hated happy. He trembled with fury. This was all Freddy's fault.

His Venomoids—three snakelike cyborgs named Twork, Babs, and Blif—slithered and hissed, curling around his arms and neck, licking his ears and bald head.

"How could-est this horribleness have-est happened?" whined Wizbad. "What ill wind hast blown-eth to make-est me not thy king?"

"I dunno," said Twork, flicking his tongue.

"No clue," said Babs, flicking *her* tongue.

"What the question?" said Blif, flicking his tongue and accidentally wrapping it around his head like a rubber band.

"Never mind, Blif!" cried Wizbad. "The main thing is that I be-est hungry. What be-est I hungry for?!"

"How 'bout a nice bowl of space-urchin soup?" whispered Babs.

"NO! NOT *SOUP*!" screamed Wizbad. "I'M HUNGRY FOR *REVENGE*!"

"Oh, right . . . revenge," said Twork and Babs.

"Okah," said Blif, "then make *me* a nice bow uh space-urcha soup."

Wizbad tipped his head wand, raised one eyebrow, and—*zap*—turned Blif into a bowl of space-urchin soup.

CLOSE CALL

"YIPPEEE, YAY, and YAHOO!" screamed Freddy and Glyzix. Flurbians on the ground looked up and cheered.

"Your public awaits!" said Glyzix.

"Okay," said Freddy. "GIZZABOOTLE, GOINK, GOINK *HOME*!"

Just then, a sleek, black, podlike airship screamed across the purple sky, swooping dangerously close to Orange Beauty. Orange Beauty flipped and rolled, tumbling out of control and into a spinning nosedive.

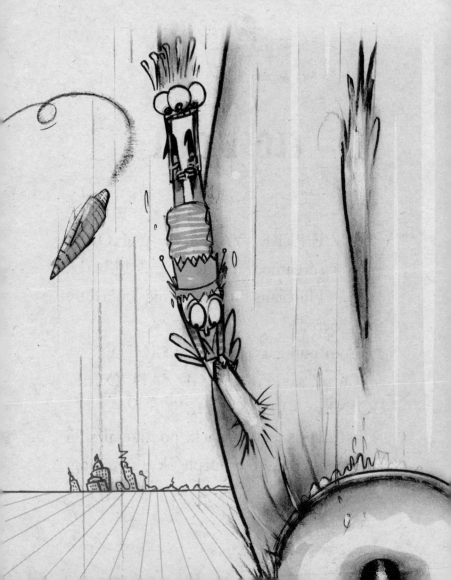

"Uh-oh," said Freddy, "we're gonna crash!"

But Glyzix was totally relaxed. "Cool it, Kingster."

And, sure enough, Orange Beauty—all ten tons of her—slowed just in the nick of time, leveled out, and landed in the palace fountain like a balloon in a bathtub.

"Who the heck was that maniac out there?" said Freddy.

"Two words," said Glyzix. "Wiz and bad."

Orange Beauty lowered her tail like an airplane emergency slide, Freddy and Glyzix rolled into the fountain, and the crowd went wild.

Freddy saw a coach leading Flurbians in oddly familiar exercises: "SQUAWK ONE! FLAP TWO! RASPBERRY THREE!

SALUTE FOUR!" Everyone was happily learning the Way of Freddy. Then a huge Freddy statue was unveiled. Freddy found it all a little embarrassing. But then he realized that maybe it wasn't so bad. Here, no one called him a nuisance or kept him after school. Everyone celebrated his Freddy-ness. They *worshipped* him.

Well, not everyone. Wizbad and the Venomoids watched the ceremony from the bush they had just crashed into. The bush had been trimmed to look like Freddy by Flurbian gardeners. Wizbad was insanely jealous.

"That should-eth be *me*," he seethed.

"Maybe if you looked more like a bush," said Babs.

"I don't *want-eth* to look like a bush!" said Wizbad, "I want-eth to destroy-eth a Freddy! But Wormola might watch-eth, so I must find someone else to do-eth the deed! Someone who hate-est the Freddy as much-eth as *I* do!"

"Don't look at me," said Blif. "Me just a bowl of soup."

FREDDY'S NUMBER
ONE FAN

Meanwhile, Mom finished polishing every crown in the crown closet. "Yippee!"

"Don't you know you should be miserable, Mom?" said Babette.

But Mom wasn't miserable. She had even found the time to make a bunch of I ♥ Freddy T-shirts.

"Mr. Supervisor, sir," she said, "may I be

excused? I'd like to start an organization called the Freddy, King of Flurb, Fantastically Fabulous Flurbian Fan Club!"

"Fantastically Fabulous!" said Zeeb.

"Yippee!"

She ran out of the palace and down the street, trying to recruit every Flurbian she met. But unfortunately, Mom was a little overenthusiastic.

"Attention, citizens!" said Mom. "Drop everything and join Freddy's Fantastically Fabulous Flurbian Fan Club. Right now, this second!"

"Sorry, Peachy Miriam," said one Flurbian pedestrian, "but I've got a full day of eating, breathing, and laughing uncontrollably ahead of me . . . basically having a life."

"Freddy *is* your life!" she said, forcing the Flurbian into a T-shirt with way too few armholes.

A huge crowd gathered and a scuffle broke out, which turned into a riot. The Flurbian guards arrived and one contacted headquarters. The call was intercepted.

"Arrest-eth Peachy Miriam for engaging in anti-Freddy activities!" said a voice.

"Who *is* this?" asked the guard.

"This be-est the Freddy himself!"

"You don't *sound* like King Freddy."

"I have-eth a cold," said you know who. "Lock-eth her up!"

THE INCREDIBLE
SHRINKING AL

Meanwhile, back at the old boot-polishing closet, Dad was hot, thirsty, and even grumpier than usual. "How come *Miriam* got to leave?"

"Miriam finished her work," said Supervisor Zeeb. "You have millions of boots left to polish."

"At least you don't have to *lick* them!" screamed Babette.

Just then, a We Love Freddy parade passed by in the street below, outside the palace gate, and, in his excitement, Zeeb forgot his duties and leaned out the window to watch.

Dad made a break for it and quickly tiptoed down the back staircase. He ran through an alley and into a Flurbian restaurant. He ordered a beverage called Gleeberpop and guzzled it down.

But then he noticed that the glass was growing larger. He looked around the room.

"What the heck is going on?!" he said to the Flurbian waiter. "You're getting taller and so is the chair! My feet don't reach the floor! They're dangling like little-kid feet!"

"Relax, Only Freddy's Father," said the waiter. "Everyone knows that Gleeberpop makes non-Flurbians shrink."

"*I* didn't know!" shrieked Dad. "How

could I know? Why would I have *ordered* it?!"

"Good question," said the waiter. "Maybe King Freddy, in his infinite wisdom, could answer that."

This made Dad even angrier. *"Infinite wisdom?!"* he squeaked. As he shrank, his voice went up in pitch. "I'm the wise one! *I* should rule Flurb!"

"But you're Only Freddy's Father!" The waiter laughed.

"Stop calling me that! My name is Al! I'm taking my case to the Furbian people!"

Dad was no bigger than a chipmunk. He made a protest sign using a fork and napkin. It said DOWN WITH FREDDY!

Then he peered over the

edge of the chair and carefully slid down one of the legs to the floor. But, before he could get his protest under way, three stupid serpentine cyborgs disguised as guards emerged from a hole in the wall.

"Stop!" yelled Twork. "You're under arrest for engaging in anti-Freddy activities!"

"Yikes!" squeaked Dad, running out the door as fast as his tiny legs could carry him.

22

BABETTE ESCAPES

Babette heard the celebration in the street below. "Wha is everthin' alwuz abbow *Fredda*?" she cried, her tongue raw and swollen from already having licked two thousand boots.

She couldn't take it anymore! She spit, trying to get the boot taste out of her mouth. She must escape! She clawed at the wall with her fingernails.

"OUCH!" said the wall. It opened up into a tunnel and Babette climbed through. She fell into the outstretched arms of Wizbad.

"So," said Wizbad, "how art-eth thou enjoying your job—it's quite an honor, you know."

"Why does everyone keep *saying* that?!" said Babette. "Back home, teachers worshipped me, boys worshipped me . . . pretty much *everyone* worshipped me. And now I'm supposed to be honored to worship my disgusting little brother? The Way of Freddy is . . . just a *very stupid way*!"

This was music to Wizbad's ears.

"Perhaps you'd like to discuss-eth this further in my chambers, Poor Babette," said Wizbad, turning and pointing his twisted finger down the hallway.

"Please don't call me that," she said, following.

Wizbad stopped. "I'm sorry, my dear. What would-est you prefer?"

"*Princess* Babette might be nice," she said.

"Princess Babette it shall-est be," said Wizbad, his mouth curling into a huge one-tooth grin as they continued down the corridor.

POOLSIDE

This was the life. Freddy and Glyzix were relaxing on gravity-defying inflatable rafts near the newly completed Freddy-shaped pool. A small refreshment robot blasted out of the royal kitchen cabana and hovered about fifteen feet in front of Freddy.

"Make your choices, blink, and say ahh," said Glyzix.

Freddy looked at the row of colorful buttons but had absolutely no idea what any of them were, so he randomly pushed a few, just by staring and blinking.

"Ahhhhh," said Freddy, opening his mouth very wide.

A nozzle flipped up and a delicious mixture of solids, liquids, and gasses gushed through the air, across the patio, and into Freddy's face. A small amount actually made it down his throat and it was by far the best thing he had ever tasted.

"Yumm," he said, smacking his lips loudly.

"Hail, Freddy, King of Flurb!" said three Flurbian sunbathers.

FROM WIZBAD
TO WIZ*WORSE*

"Here, Princess Babette," said Wizbad, "sit-est thou in my comfy cloud chair."

"Thanks, Wizzy," said Babette, easing into the cozy floating cushion.

"Let's talk more about the Freddy and how you hate his guts," whispered Wizbad.

"Well, I wouldn't exactly say *hate* . . ." she said.

Wizbad tilted his head wand and zapped her, casting a spell. He twisted her real feelings into something uglier.

"Oooh, ouch, yes," she said, wincing. "Come to think of it, I hate his guts with great enthusiasm."

"What would-eth you do to bring him down?" he said, zapping her again.

"What *wouldn't* I do?" she mumbled, her eyes rolling back in her head.

Wizbad dressed Babette up like Freddy and put a crown on her head. He gently pushed the cloud chair across the room and out onto a balcony that overlooked the main Flurbian square, where a gigantic crowd was assembled, still waiting to meet Freddy. Wizbad knew that from far away, the Flurbians would never be able to tell the difference between Freddy and Babette.

Wizbad whispered in Babette's ear: "Okay, Princess, this is your chance to get back at that bratty brother. See-est those dimwitted Flurbians down there? They think-eth you are the Freddy. All you need-eth to do is play along and say a few words in-eth the voice of the Freddy that will make them lose faith in the Freddy's leadership. Get-eth it? It's really quite-eth simple."

"Hmmm . . ." said Babette, "I believe I can handle that."

Wizbad threw the switch on a loud-speaker.

"Greetings, Flurbians," said Babette. "This is Freddy, your leader. I am here to say that I am a total screw-up. I am not qualified to rule anything or anyone."

The crowd was stunned.

Wizbad whispered in her ear again: "Good, Princess. Now think of something for the Freddy to say-eth about *Flurb* and *Flurbians* that would really make-eth them *hate* him."

Babette thought for a moment.

"Hello again, everyone!" she continued. "I forgot to mention that all Flurbians are smelly, ugly nincompoops! And—if the universe gave out an annual award for the worst, most horrible planet, Flurb would win every year. With five arms tied behind its back!"

That was the last straw. At that exact moment the crowd became a mob.

Flurbians are very patriotic.

"Down with King Freddy!" cried one.

"Turns out he's a slacker *and* a slob!" cried another.

Wizbad pulled Babette in from the balcony and addressed the crowd.

"Fellow Flurbians!" he cried, "Freddy, King of Flurb, has left-eth the building! He is heading in the direction of the fancy new-eth Freddy-shaped pool! Boy, was *that* a waste-eth of time and money!"

"GET HIM!!!!" roared the mob as they stormed off.

"Well, Princess Babette," he said, "that was helpful . . . very helpful. Thank you from-eth the bottom of my . . . well, not my heart, because I don't have-eth one. Had a chest X-ray once and it turns out I've got-eth a heart-shaped void down-est there. It is quite fascinating. But, anyway, thanks."

"You're quite welcome," said Babette, who was coming out of her trance. "And now I hope you'll see it in your heart-shaped void to help *me*. I've got a prom to catch."

"Yes! No problem! Have-eth a nice trip!" said Wizbad, turning to leave. "I've got a *throne* to catch!"

In marched a huge guard.

"You're here to take me home!" gushed Babette.

"Not quite," he said. "I'm here to take you to the dungeon for your anti-Freddy activities. King Freddy's orders."

"Excuse me?" said Babette.

The guard pushed a serpent-shaped lever and the chamber wall opened. The wall's mouth swallowed Babette before she had time to scream. She heard the guard laugh as she slid down the hatch.

"You're gonna love the poison-quilled rat toads," he called after her.

Babette tumbled through an intestine-like tunnel and was deposited onto a bunk in a certain jail cell. She and her parents

were surrounded by dozens of growling little critters.

"Don't tell me," she said, "poison-quilled rat toads."

One rat toad screeched, hopped up, and hurled a volley of quills at Babette. She ducked and they stuck into the wall behind her.

"*Grumble, grumble, peep!*" said Dad from his perch. He was now the size of a canary, and was locked inside a birdcage.

"Freddy has gone mad with *peep*—I mean *power*!" said Dad.

"I have to admit," said Mom, "this is no way to treat one's mother. Or even one's crown polisher, for that matter." She looked down at the I ♥ Freddy T-shirt she had on over her dress. She took it off, revealing another one. It turned out she had put on all the I ♥ Freddy shirts. With tears in her eyes, she pulled them off and ripped them to shreds.

POOL PARTY'S OVER

Meanwhile, Freddy, Glyzix, and the three Flurbian sunbathers lounged at the Freddy-shaped pool.

Glyzix climbed the ladder to the high diving board. He was little more than a speck against the chartreuse Flurbian sky. Freddy watched him hurtling toward the ground and at the last second, Glyzix struck a series of crazy poses, pulled himself completely inside

himself, and cannonballed into the water.

This made a huge tidal wave. Every last drop of water came out of the pool, soaking Freddy and the sunbathers and making them laugh.

But the sunbathers' laughter struck Freddy as odd: "Ssss, sssss, sssss, sssss!" They pulled their arms to their sides and hunched their shoulders. They hunched higher and higher until their shoulders fused with their heads and their arms fused with their bodies. Their legs became thick tails. They hissed and flicked their tongues and quickly coiled around and around Freddy, tightening and squeezing, tying themselves into one big knot with Freddy at its center. Freddy couldn't move. He could barely breathe.

"So, who are you really?" gasped Freddy.

Blif spoke up: "He's Twork, she's Babs, and I used to be a bowl of soup, but I got better."

That's when the angry mob arrived. They roared and screamed every imaginable insult at Freddy.

"I can't believe we used to *worship* this

108

jerk!" said an angry Flurbian.

"Freddy, Ex-king of Flurb!" said another.

"Do I get to keep the me-shaped pool?" said Freddy.

Just then a huge government truck backed up and dumped about forty tons of cement into the pool.

"Stop!" cried Freddy. "*Glyzix* is in there!"

"Nice try," said Blif. "Whadya thinks we is, stupid?"

"Don't answer that," said Twork. "To the Flurbian maximum security dungeon! Pronto!" They stormed off to the dungeon and threw Freddy into a very, very, *very* depressing cell.

DOING DUNGEON TIME

The bunk in Freddy's cell was hard. It was just a large space rock. The pillow was a small space rock. The alarm clock was a space rock on a stick. Freddy was miserable.

Glyzix was gone. And where was Freddy's family? He hoped they'd find out he was in the dungeon and come rescue him. He wondered what they thought of him *now*.

"That Freddy," said Babette. "What a no-good slacker."

Wow, thought Freddy, *not exactly what I'd hoped for, but I sure have a good imagination.*

"That Freddy," said Dad. "What a no-good slob."

Holy cow, Freddy thought, *his voice is squeakier than usual, but it almost sounds like he's right next door.*

When he heard his mom's voice, he realized they *were* right next door.

"Anyone want to join the Freddy Sure Is a Total Jerk club?" she whimpered.

Freddy couldn't believe his ears. Apparently his mom's so-called infinite love had run out. Everyone hated him.

27

FREDDY WHO?

reddy called to them: "Hey! Over there! Mom! Dad! Babette even! It's me, Freddy!"

"Sorry, we don't know a Freddy," said Mom.

"What exactly are you so mad about?!" he asked.

"Let's see," said Babette. "You got us abducted, turned into slaves, and thrown into a depressing dungeon, where we're about to be quilled to death by a gaggle of grotesque rat toads!"

Freddy wondered what the heck she was talking about, but just then the floor started moving under Freddy's feet, opening like a sliding door. Huge purple flames shot up. Freddy backed up against the opposite wall.

"MOM! DAD! BABETTE!" he screamed.

The wall to Freddy's right started to rumble and open up. A large green tongue stuck out and standing on its tip was Glyzix. He squashed down inside himself and flipped into the cell. He had gone down the drain in the pool and made his way through miles of underground passageways to find Freddy.

"C'mon, Kingster," said Glyzix. "I'll lead you to safety."

"Thanks, Glyz," said Freddy, "but I can't desert my family, even if they do kinda hate me."

"Don't be silly," shouted Babette, "we *really* hate you!"

The opening created by the sliding floor was getting closer and closer to Freddy and Glyzix, and the flames curled around them.

The passageway that Glyzix had come through was now engulfed in flames.

Then the ceiling opened.

"What now?" said Freddy.

Down through a hatch came a free-floating glass pod. Inside was Wizbad and his serpentine cyborgs. Blif laughed, spattering flecks of venom onto the glass.

"Gee," said Babs. "The Freddy be trapped by smokiness and flamey-ness."

"Yeah . . . ," said Blif. "Should we *helps* the Freddy?"

"Yes-eth," hissed Wizbad sarcastically, "I think-eth I'll just let-eth him go now."

"Really?!" said Blif.

"NOOOO!" howled Wizbad. "Bad guys don't help-eth good guys! Have you even

bothered to read the bad-guy rule book I bought you?!" He glared at Freddy. "Listen, you . . . I am sick-eth and tired of being second in command, second banana, second whatever! From now on I'm going to be *first* whatever! Because I be-est a *real* king . . . a cruel and creepy king. *Cruel-eepy,* if you will! And I have a cruel-eepy plan. Little old me will be-eth king and little old everyone else will be-eth slaves! Except little old you will be-eth dead!" His fang glistened. Rivers of sweat ran down his blood-red face and hot green lava leaked from one ear.

Freddy looked at Glyzix. "That Wizbad is one cruel-eepy nut job," he whispered. "I gotta think. It is the duty of a great leader to think clearly and get tough in tough situations."

"I hate to break it to you, Kingster," said Glyzix, "but you have no time to think *or*

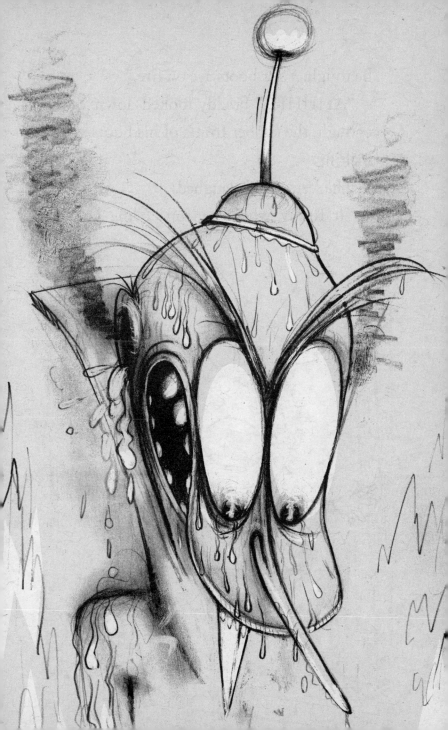

be tough. Your boots are on fire."

"AHHHH!" Freddy looked down. Sure enough, the rubber fronts of his boots were melting.

The Venomoids laughed.

"It funny when someone being hurted

when it not *me* being hurted." Blif chuckled.

Freddy was scared. But sometimes fear is a good motivator, and an idea popped into his head. He put his fingers in the corners of his mouth and took a very deep breath. He let loose with the loudest, most fantastic Squawking, Flapping, Atomic-Raspberry-Chicken Salute ever.

He followed that with a fast, then slow, then fast series of Bionic Belches and Gassy Whistles: *"BURRRRRRR-EEP-EEP-EEP-BLAMMO-BLAMMO-EEP-EEP-BURRRRR-EEP! TWEET-TWEET-ZZZZZOP-HOOTY-HOOT-KABOOM-BOOM!"*

And something new: the screaming, yelling Big Fat Asteroid. *"KERRRRRRRRRRR-ZOINK-A-MA-BLAM!"*

"I hate-eth to interrupt whatever that is you're doing," said Wizbad, "but your pants are on fire."

Freddy looked down and, sure enough, his pants were on fire. He was not a liar . . . his pants really were on fire. But that didn't stop him. He did forty-two variations on the Flurbian Flabberblaster: *"ZIP-ZIP-FLABBO-FLABBO-FLURBO-FLURBO-BOOM!!!"* And then he stopped.

"Thank-eth goodness *that's* over," said Wizbad. "It was driving me absolutely bonkers."

"Tell me about it," called Babette from next door. "I have to live with that guy."

But Freddy hadn't just been making silly noises. . . .

Suddenly the jail cell started rumbling. Then came a great groaning and creaking from deep inside the dungeon. The building started rocking and heaving. Wizbad's glass pod bounced and spun, swinging wildly through the flames that leaped higher and higher. Lava spurted from Wizbad's ears.

Wizbad and the Venomoids cried like teeny-tiny babies.

Glyzix and Freddy's family were also terrified.

But Freddy wasn't. He had used those idiotic sounds—from that day forward known as the Royal Code of Freddy—to send a set of complicated instructions to a friend:

Hi, how are you?
I've got a teeny favor to ask.
1. Take a little trip to your friendly Flurbian hardware store and pick up the following items . . . blah, blah, blah . . .
2. Don't forget to stop off at beautiful Lake Flurb.
3. Swing around and pick up your cousin.

As you know, he will take some coaxing.
4. Hurry. My pants are on fire . . . AND
I'M NOT LYING!
Thanks in advance,
Freddy, King of Flurb

Suddenly, the breathing walls, the heaving ceiling, the entire Flurbian maximum security dungeon lifted up off its foundation.

Orange Beauty—using an amazing system of chains and pulleys (recently purchased at a Flurbian hardware store) and the muscles and machinery of her biomechanical body—coaxed her cousin (the dungeon) to his or its feet. "Thanks, cousin!" said the dungeon, having been in that position for several centuries and really needing a stretch.

"Man, I love this crazy planet," said Freddy.

The dungeon's legs were a bit wobbly,

causing Wizbad to jerk forward. His fang—which had gotten really sharp—clinked into the glass wall of the pod and got stuck. This made a tiny crack that quickly spread until the pod was covered in spiderweb-like cracks. When Wizbad yanked his tooth back out, it broke in half and the glass shattered into trillions of pieces.

The bad guys fell into the fire, as Wizbad's ears spewed lava and small flaming boulders in all directions.

"Hey," screamed Blif. "I said it funny when it *not* me being hurted!"

Suddenly, a tidal wave of water, the entire contents of Lake Flurb, rushed from Orange Beauty's gigantic mouth and crashed down on everything, immediately putting out the fire and saving everyone—including Wizbad and the Venomoids, who were somewhat steamed, roasted, and toasted . . . but alive.

Freddy called to his family, "Are you all right over there?!"

"Oh, just fine," said Babette, "except for the . . . OUCH-QUILLED! OOCH-TOADS!"

Freddy shouted a command to Orange Beauty, who quickly lowered her tail escalator, breaking down the wall between the two cells. Mom, Babette, and Glyzix hopped on. Freddy grabbed the birdcage containing Dad and followed close behind.

As they took off, Freddy looked out over the entire kingdom of Flurb. The citizens waved up at him and cheered. Flurbians do not hold a grudge and they were back to being huge Freddy fans. The Royal Band

struck up the Flurbian national anthem.

Wizbad, realizing he had lost this round, made a show of patching things up with Freddy. "Yoo-hoo, King Freddy!" he called from the ground, "I am soooo-eth sorry that we got off on the wrong-eth foot. Let me take-eth this opportunity to say that I regret the horrible mix-eth-up that caused all this unpleasantness, and I pledge-eth to be the very best second whatever *ever*. Citizens of Flurb . . . join-eth me in renewing our loyalty to our one true-eth leader, the exalted, the exceedingly kingly, what a guy . . . Freddy, King of Flurb!"

Freddy rolled his eyes. He didn't fall for that at all. But somehow, the Flurbians—being a bit too trusting—did. Plus, Wizbad cast a spell of forgetfulness on the entire population. No one even noticed the bulging purple veins in Wizbad's yellow eyes or the steaming stream of green lava trickling down his neck. He leaned in close to the Venomoids and pledged his eternal hate for Freddy.

"Mark my words," he hissed, "I will never, ever, ever, ever rest-eth until I taste sweet, sweet . . ."

"Yootleturds?" said all three Venomoids.

Wizbad tilted his head wand, raised an eyebrow, and—*poof*—turned them into a pile of yootleturds.

Mom, of course, showered Freddy with love. "It had never run out," she said. "I just put it on hold during that whole poison-quilled-rat-toad business."

This was all very bittersweet for Dad. The effects of the Gleeberpop wore off and he was back to normal size, but his head remained stuck inside the birdcage.

Babette was happy to be alive but

unhappy about almost everything else.

"Well, Kingster," said Glyzix, "how was that for your first day?"

"Piece of yootleturd cake," said Freddy.

"Good," said Glyzix, "because I've just been informed that one of our bloodthirsty neighbors is plotting something very, very, very evil."

"Sorry," said Babette. "Freddy can't be king anymore, because we're going back home where everything will be about *me* again. Right, Freddy?"

"Right," said Freddy. "Except that I did promise to serve and protect the citizens of Flurb. Plus, I gotta say . . . I kinda like being worshipped." He made the *click-click* sound that a rider makes to a horse.

"NO!" screamed Babette.

"WHAT! WHAT! WHAT!" grumbled Dad.

"YIPPEE!" squealed Mom.

Orange Beauty reared back as if standing on her hind legs in midair.

"What are you waiting for?" said Glyzix.

"*GIZZABOOTLE, GIZZABOOTLE— GOINK, GOINK, GOINK!*" hollered Freddy.

Orange Beauty whinnied and took off like a turbocharged racehorse. Freddy, Glyzix, Mom, Dad, and Babette screamed and held on for dear life, but soon their screams turned into nervous laughter; then nearly normal laughter; and finally pure, uncontrollable laughter as they did forty-seven barrel rolls at the speed of light over the city and into the red-purple-chartreuse Flurbian sunset.

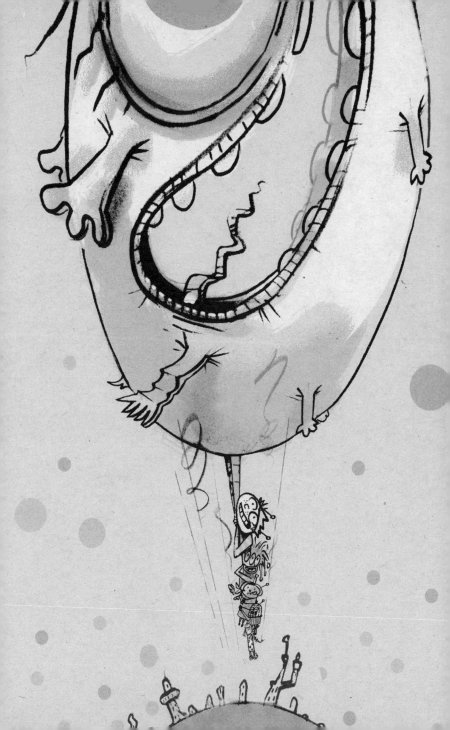

Don't miss Freddy's next adventure on Flurb!

FLURBIAN JOYRIDE

A bright orange blur streaked and looped across the purple Flurbian sky. It took a sharp downward turn and then shot straight up again. Screaming and yelling rang out across the multicolored landscape, but it quickly turned into laughter . . . uncontrollable laughter.

It was King Freddy and Glyzix riding Orange Beauty on a high-speed tour of the Flurbian wilderness. Freddy's crown flew off his head, and Glyzix immediately replaced it with another. It was the eleventh crown Freddy had lost that afternoon, but it was totally worth it.

Now the seven Flurbian suns were about to set. "We'd better head home, Kingster," said Glyzix. "On Flurb, when the suns go down—"

"I know, I know," said Freddy. "They go down *fast*." As if on cue, the suns suddenly dropped like stones beyond the far hills, plunging Flurb into total darkness.

Just as suddenly, Orange Beauty turned downward in a wild death plunge.

"AHHHHHH!" yelled Freddy.

2

"C'mon, O.B."—Glyzix yawned—"you're going to scare our young ruler out of his wits."

Orange Beauty's eyeball lit up like a headlight. The ground was closer than Freddy thought.

"AHHHHHHH *AGAIN*!" he yelled.

But just when it looked like they were about to be flattened on the rocky Flurbian surface, the ground opened up and they plunged into one of Flurb's many underground canals. Freddy closed his mouth and held his breath as they went deep into the water, but before he knew it, they popped back up to the surface and were all laughing again. The canal twisted and turned and dipped and dropped like the wildest water park ride in the universe. What a planet.

A HEAVY MESSAGE

By the time Freddy and Glyzix slid down Orange Beauty's tail, the whole palace was asleep. Not just the residents—the palace *itself* was asleep . . . and snoring.

"Good night, Kingster," said Glyzix, shaking blue sand from his head plumes. Then he yawned, scrunched inside himself, and blasted off like a spring-loaded rocket to his room.

Freddy entered the royal sleeping chambers and looked over at his bed, which was gigantic, bigger than his entire house on Earth. In fact, it was so big he had created a bed within a bed that became his cozy, private getaway. The mattress was covered with all Freddy's stuff—gadgets, comic books, leftover birthday cake. His birthday had been a couple of days ago. Everyone in the kingdom had given him amazing presents—stuff he couldn't have even imagined back on Earth. And his parents had given Freddy the only thing they had. It was a tiny flashlight that Dad had grabbed off his nightstand when they were being abducted. It said JOE'S HARDWARE on it, and, though it wasn't much, it was Freddy's favorite gift. Mostly because it was from his parents and it reminded him of home. Babette, on the other hand, hadn't given him anything. "I'll give you a birthday present when you get me off this stupid planet," she'd said.

Freddy brushed his teeth and washed his face (actually, his personal-hygiene robot did it for him). Then he took off across the floor toward the hovering Flurbian-style trampoline that he used to jump onto the bed. He was in midair when he heard it—a high-pitched whine that sounded like an incoming missile. Freddy immediately tucked and rolled and slid *under* the bed for protection, just as a large meteorite crashed through the arched bedroom ceiling, through Freddy's bed—slicing off the points of Freddy's crown as it passed—and through the floor. Freddy heard a gigantic crash down below, and then the low, rumbling voice of the palace said one word: "Ouch." Freddy looked down the hole and saw that the boulder had blown through four more floors on the way to its final resting

place in Orange Beauty's stall, located directly below his room. The gigantic green rock had landed right on the royal steed's tail, but it hadn't woken her up. Orange Beauty could sleep through anything.

Everybody else was jolted awake though, and Freddy's mom was the first to enter his bedroom. She saw the gaping hole and imagined the worst.

"MY FREDDY! MY ADORABLE LITTLE FREDDY, KING OF FLURB!"

"I'm okay, Mom," replied Freddy from under the bed, but she couldn't hear him over her own screaming.

"DISASTER! WOE IS ME! WOE IS FLURB!"

Babette shuffled in and put her hand over her mother's mouth. "I have a feeling your precious little brat king may have survived this incident," she said.

"How do you know?" Mom asked between sobs.

"Because I can see him under the bed, which is exactly eighteen times the size of my whole bed*room*, by the way."

"How can you think of bed size at a time like this?" said Mom.

"Uh, guys," said Freddy, wriggling out from under the bed. "Huge hole here."

Freddy led the way and everyone followed him down to the stables. Wizbad was already there, and he had found a large envelope tied to the boulder.

"Well," said Wizbad, "what have-est we here?"

"It look-eth like-eth a rock-eth and an envelope-eth," mocked Freddy. He loved to make fun of the way Wizbad spoke. He knew it wasn't very nice, but Wizbad wasn't very nice either. He was basically an evil,

greedy, all-around pain in the nergzip.

"Very amusing-eth," said Wizbad, trying
to hide the fact that he hated Freddy more
than anything in the universe. Literally. More

than *anything*. Once he had gotten a splinter in his eye from a Flurbian fire-spice tree, and even that hadn't bothered him half as much as Freddy. He blamed Freddy for everything, including his broken fang. It caused him excruciating pain—but Wizbad refused to get it repaired because he *liked* being reminded of his hate for Freddy. He was just that nuts.

Still, Wizbad had to be very careful not to make his real feelings known. First, because the Flurbian people absolutely adored Freddy. And, second, because Ex-king Wormola (now enjoying his retirement . . . fishing for space trout, playing space bingo, whatever) had chosen Freddy as his replacement and was watching from afar, keeping an eye on the diabolical wizard.

Wizbad opened the envelope. He pulled out a handheld scanner translator and read the message:

"'Greetings, Freddy, King of Flurb—

"'Welcome to the neighborhood. We, the undersigned, hate you. The attached rock is a symbol of that hate. We hoped it would land on you and squash you, but if you're reading this, it obviously didn't, so we'd like to take this opportunity to say (and please scream as loudly as possible when you read this):

"'GET OUT OF THE GALAXY AND TAKE YOUR LAME-O FAMILY WITH YOU! . . . OR FACE OUR WRATH, EARTH DORK!

"'And by "wrath" we mean the immediate invasion of Flurb and a public pulverizing of you and your family and the rest of the population with the brand-new industrial-sized pulverizer we just ordered from a catalog. It was a pretty good deal—we split the cost three ways.

"'Sincerely yours—

"'Chewtyke, Supreme Leader of Molaria

"'Big Bad Wongo, *Supreme-er* Leader of Wongolia

"'Deathsnail, *Supreme-est* Leader of Z-9X G-Vector.'"

"Catchy name for a planet," said Freddy.

"Freddy!" screeched Babette. "Being pulverized would seriously cramp my style, once we get off this stupid planet. By the way . . . do you know what time it is?"

"No," said Mom.

"IT'S TIME FOR US TO GET THE HECK OFF THIS STUPID PLANET!" screamed Babette.

Don't miss any of Freddy's adventures in space!

Freddy and his family have been abducted by aliens! Next stop, the planet Flurb, where things couldn't be more different from their ordinary life on Earth. On Flurb the aliens make Freddy KING and everyone worships him! Well, maybe not everyone. Not the vicious leaders of nearby planets, who want to publicly pulverize him, not his scheming sister, Babette, who can't stand being ruled by him, and certainly not the superjealous Wizbad, who will stop at nothing to knock Freddy from his throne!

HARPER

An Imprint of HarperCollinsPublishers

www.harpercollinschildrens.com